1995

Happy

Love,

Dad & Mom

W9-AYA-293

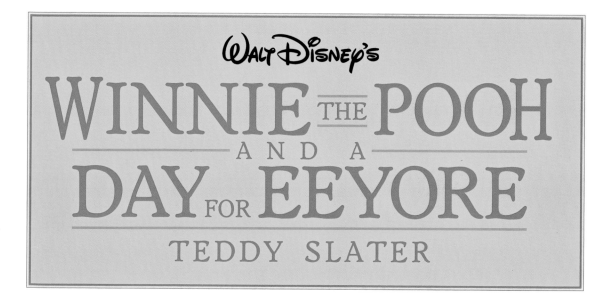

Walt Disney's
WINNIE THE POOH
AND A
DAY FOR EEYORE

TEDDY SLATER

ILLUSTRATED BY
BILL LANGLEY AND JOHN KURTZ

Disney PRESS

New York

Copyright © 1994 by Disney Press.
All rights reserved.
No part of this book may be used or reproduced in any manner whatsoever
without written permission from the publisher.
Printed and bound in the United States of America.
For information address Disney Press,
114 Fifth Avenue, New York, New York 10011.
Based on the Pooh stories by A. A. Milne (copyright The Pooh Properties Trust).

First Edition
1 3 5 7 9 10 8 6 4 2

Library of Congress Catalog Card Number: 94-70810
ISBN: 1-56282-657-3

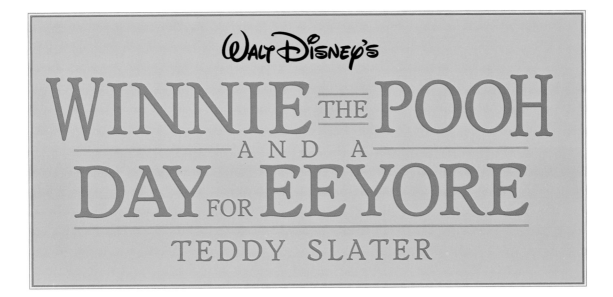

Walt Disney's

WINNIE THE POOH AND A DAY FOR EEYORE

TEDDY SLATER

$\mathscr{A}$T THE EDGE OF THE HUNDRED-ACRE WOOD, a lovely old bridge crossed a peaceful little river. Now, this bridge was a favorite spot of Winnie the Pooh's, and he would often wander there, doing nothing in particular and thinking nothing in particular. But on one such wandering, something suddenly took Pooh's mind off of nothing. And that something was a big brown pinecone, which dropped—*PLOP!*—right on his head.

Pooh picked up the pinecone and gazed at it thoughtfully. As he walked along, he decided to make up a little poem. But while his head was occupied (he was trying to think of a word that rhymed with *cone*), his feet, left to their own devices, tripped over a tree root, and Pooh tumbled to the ground.

Pooh kept on tumbling until he came to a stop on the bridge just as the pinecone went skittering over the edge and into the water below.

"Oh bother," said Pooh. "I suppose I shall have to find another one."

Now, Pooh had every intention of doing just that. But the river was slipping away so peacefully beneath him that his thoughts began to slip away with it.

"That's funny," Pooh said to himself as the pinecone drifted under the bridge and floated lazily downstream. "I dropped it on one side, and it came out on the other.

"Hmm . . .," he murmured, also to himself. "I wonder if it would do that again."

So he collected a rather large and a rather small pinecone and tossed them over the far side of the bridge. Then he scurried to the other side and waited.

"I wonder which one will come out first," said Pooh.

Well, as it turned out, the big one came out first, and the little one came out last, which was just what Pooh had hoped. And that was the beginning of a game called Pooh Sticks, named for its inventor—Winnie the Pooh.

Now, you might think it should have been called Pooh *Cones*, but since it was easier to collect a handful of sticks than an armful of cones, Pooh made a slight improvement on his original game.

And so it came to pass that one fine day Pooh, Piglet, Rabbit, and Roo were all on the bridge playing Pooh Sticks.

"All right now," Rabbit said. "The first stick to pass all the way under the bridge wins. On your mark, get set . . . go!"

Pooh, Piglet, Rabbit, and Roo all threw their sticks into the water. Then they raced to the other side of the bridge to see whose would come out first.

"I can see mine," Roo shouted, pointing to a short black stick in the water. "I win! I win!" he cried, even as the "stick" suddenly spread its wings and flew off to join the other dragonflies flitting about.

"Can you see yours, Pooh?" Piglet asked, peering down at the gently flowing river.

"No," Pooh said. "I expect my stick's stuck."

"They always take longer than you think," Rabbit assured him just as something long, gray, and quite sticklike floated into view.

"Oh, I can see yours, Piglet," Pooh cried.

"Are you sure it's mine?" Piglet asked doubtfully.

"Sure," said Roo, "it's a gray one. A very big gray one."

"Oh, no, it isn't," said Rabbit. "It's . . . it's . . ."

"Eeyore!" everyone shouted.

"Don't pay any attention to me," Eeyore muttered as he floated by his friends, tail first. "Nobody ever does."

Rabbit leaned over the bridge. "Eeyore," he cried. "What are you doing down there?"

"I'll give you three guesses," Eeyore said flatly.

"Fishing?" asked Pooh.

"Wrong," said Eeyore.

"Going for a sail?" Roo guessed.

"Wrong again!"

"Ah, waiting for somebody to help you out of the river?" Rabbit tried.

"That's right," Eeyore mumbled more or less to himself. "Give Rabbit the time and he'll get the answer."

Piglet looked down at his friend in alarm. "Eeyore," he cried, "what can we . . . I mean, how should we . . . do you think if we . . ."

"Yes," Eeyore said calmly, "one of those would be just the thing. Thank you, Piglet."

"I've got an idea," Pooh offered hesitantly. "But I don't suppose it's a very good one."

"I don't suppose it is," Eeyore gurgled as his head tipped beneath the water.

"Go on, Pooh," Rabbit urged. "Let's have it."

"Well," Pooh said, "if we all threw stones and things into the river on one side of Eeyore, the stones would make waves, and the waves would wash him to the other side."

"That's a fine idea," said Rabbit. "I'm glad we thought of it, Pooh." But Pooh had already gone off to find a suitable stone.

Eeyore floated around and around in a circle until finally Pooh reappeared, rolling a great big boulder onto the bridge.

Rabbit immediately took charge. "Piglet," he directed, "give Pooh a little more room. Roo, get back a bit." And to Pooh he said, "I think a little to the left. No, no, a little to the right."

It took a while, but Pooh finally got the stone lined up to Rabbit's satisfaction. "Pooh," Rabbit said then, "when I say 'Now,' you can drop it."

Then he turned to Eeyore, "When I say 'Now,' Pooh will drop the stone. Are you ready . . . ?

"One . . . ," Rabbit counted. "Two . . . ," and "now!" he cried.

And with that, Pooh gave a mighty heave that sent the boulder off the bridge—and right smack on top of Eeyore!

"Oh dear," Pooh sighed as Eeyore sank out of sight. "Perhaps it wasn't such a very good idea after all."

Pooh was still peering woefully at the spot where his friend had disappeared when Eeyore came sloshing out of the water and onto the riverbank.

"Oh, Eeyore," Piglet squealed. "You're all wet."

"That happens when you've been in a river a long time," Eeyore said, shaking himself dry and giving Piglet a bit of a bath in the process.

"How did you fall in the river, Eeyore?" Rabbit asked.

"I didn't *fall* in," Eeyore said. "I was *bounced* in! I was just sitting by the side of the river, minding my own business, when I received a loud bounce."

"But who did it?" Pooh wanted to know.

"I expect it was T-Tigger," Piglet replied.

The words were no sooner out of Piglet's mouth than Tigger himself bounced onto the scene and knocked Rabbit flat on his back!

"Eeyore," Rabbit said, scrambling to his feet, "was it Tigger who bounced you?"

"I didn't bounce him," said Tigger. "I happened to be behind Eeyore and I . . . I simply coughed."

"You bounced me," Eeyore said accusingly.

"I didn't bounce," Tigger repeated. "I coughed."

"Bouncing or coughing," Eeyore said, "it's all the same."

"Oh no it's not," Tigger insisted.

But after several more rounds of "Bounced!" "Coughed!" "Did not!" "Did too!" Tigger finally admitted that he had in fact bounced Eeyore into the water.

"It was just a joke," he said sheepishly. But no one was laughing, least of all Eeyore.

"Some people have no sense of humor," Tigger grumbled as he went bouncing off into the woods.

"Tigger is so thoughtless," Rabbit said.

"Why should Tigger think of me?" Eeyore said. "No one else does."

"Why do you say that, Eeyore?" Pooh asked, but Eeyore was already shambling away, head hung, shoulders drooping.

Eeyore followed the stream back to his Gloomy Spot. As he sat there under what seemed to be his very own rain cloud, he could see his sad face in the water. "Pathetic," Eeyore said to his reflection.

Eeyore lumbered around to the other side of the bank and peered into the water again. "Just as I thought," he said. "No better from here. Pa-thetic," he repeated.

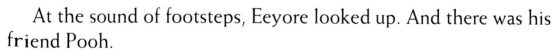

At the sound of footsteps, Eeyore looked up. And there was his friend Pooh.

"Eeyore," Pooh said softly. "What's the matter?"

"What makes you think anything's the matter?" Eeyore sighed.

"You seem so sad," said Pooh.

"Why should I be sad?" Eeyore asked sadly. And then, answering his own question, he said, "It's my birthday. The happiest day of the year."

"Your birthday?" Pooh said, surprised.

"Of course," Eeyore said. "Can't you see the presents?"

"No," Pooh replied, looking around in confusion.

"Can't you see the cake?" Eeyore went on. "The candles and the pink icing?"

"Well, no," Pooh said, more confused than before.

"Neither can I," Eeyore said with a sigh.

"Oh," said Pooh. Not quite sure what to say next, he said, "Well, many happy returns of the day, Eeyore."

"Thank you, Pooh," Eeyore said. "But we can't all. . . . And some of us don't."

"Can't all what?" Pooh asked.

"No gaiety," Eeyore intoned. "No song and dance. No 'Here We Go Round the Mulberry Bush.' But don't worry about me, Pooh," he said. "Go and enjoy yourself. I'll stay here and be miserable, with no presents, no cake, and no candles. . . ."

As Eeyore's mournful voice trailed off, Pooh gently patted him on the back and said, "Eeyore, wait right here." Then he hurried off as fast as he could.

When Pooh got home, he found Piglet jumping up and down at the door, trying desperately to reach the door knocker.

"Here, let me do it," said Pooh, lifting the knocker.

"B-but Pooh—," Piglet started.

"I found out what's troubling Eeyore," Pooh interrupted. "It's his birthday, and nobody has taken any notice of it."

Pooh looked at the still-closed door. "Well, whoever lives here certainly takes a long time to answer the door."

"But Pooh, isn't this . . . your house?" asked Piglet.

"Oh, so it is," answered Pooh.

As the two friends went inside, Pooh declared, "I must get poor Eeyore a present. But what?" he wondered, looking around for a likely gift.

Just then Pooh spied a small honeypot in the pantry. "Ah, honey," he cried. "That should do very well." And turning to Piglet, he said, "What are you giving Eeyore?"

For a moment poor Piglet seemed quite at a loss, but then he said, "Perhaps I could give Eeyore a balloon."

"That," said Pooh, "is a very good idea!"

"I have one at home," Piglet exclaimed. "I'll go and get it right now."

So off Piglet hurried in one direction, and off Pooh went in the other.

Pooh hadn't gone far when a funny feeling crept over him. It began at the very tip of his nose and trickled all the way down to his toes. It was as if someone inside him were saying, "Now then, Pooh, time for a little something."

So Pooh reached into the honeypot and had a little something. Then he had a little more, and still a little more. And before long he had licked the honeypot clean.

As Pooh absentmindedly wiped the last sticky drop from his mouth, he said, "Now, where was I going? Oh, yes, Eeyore. I was. . . ." And looking down at the empty jar he said, "Oh bother, I must give Eeyore something."

But first, Pooh decided, he'd go visit his good friend Owl.

Owl was busy hanging a picture of his great-uncle Robert on the wall when Pooh knocked at the door.

"Many happy returns of Eeyore's birthday," Pooh said.

"You know, that reminds me of a birthday of my great-uncle Robert," Owl said, waving Pooh in with one wing and pointing to the newly hung portrait with the other.

"Uncle Robert had just reached the ripe old age of one hundred and three," Owl explained, "though of course he would only admit to ninety-seven. We all felt a celebration was in order, so . . ."

"What are you giving him?" Pooh broke in the moment Owl
paused for breath.

"Giving who?" Owl asked, peering quizzically at Pooh.

"Eeyore," Pooh replied.

"Oh, Eeyore," Owl chuckled. "Of course! I, ah . . . Well, what are
you giving him, Pooh?"

"I'm giving him this useful pot to keep things in," said Pooh,
holding out the empty honeypot, "and I—"

"A useful pot?" said Owl, peering into the jar. "Evidently some-one has been keeping honey in it."

"Yes," said Pooh. "It's very useful like that, but I wanted to ask you—"

"You ought to write 'Happy Birthday' on it," said Owl.

"That was what I wanted to ask you," explained Pooh. "My own spelling is a bit wobbly."

"Very well," Owl said. And he took the pot and his pen and got down to work. "It's easier if people don't look while I'm writing," he added, turning his back on Pooh.

After what seemed a rather long time, Owl turned around again. "There!" he said, proudly holding up the pot. "All finished. What do you think of it?"

"It looks like a lot of words just to say 'Happy Birthday,'" Pooh pointed out.

"Well, actually, I wrote 'A Very Happy Birthday, with Love from Pooh,'" Owl explained. "Naturally it takes a good deal of words to say something like that."

"Oh, I see," Pooh said, taking the pot. "Thank you, Owl."

While Pooh went to deliver his gift to Eeyore, Owl headed off to Christopher Robin's house. On the way, he flew directly over Piglet, who was running along with a big red balloon.

"Many happy returns of Eeyore's birthday, Piglet," Owl hollered down.

"Many happy returns to you, too, Owl," Piglet hollered up.

But as Piglet hollered up, he neglected to look down and ran smack into a tree.

Piglet bounced off the tree and came to a stop—*POP!*—right on top of what *had been* the big red balloon.

"Oh d-d-dear. How shall I? What shall I? Well . . . maybe Eeyore doesn't like balloons so very much," Piglet said.

So he trudged off to Eeyore's, dragging the remains of the balloon behind him. Piglet found his friend moping under a leafless tree.

"Many happy returns of the day," Piglet sang out.

"Meaning my birthday," Eeyore said glumly.

"Yes," said Piglet. "And I've brought you a present."

"Pardon me, Piglet," Eeyore said, perking up. "My hearing must be going. I thought you said you brought me a present."

"I did," said Piglet. "I brought you a b-balloon."

"Balloon?" Eeyore echoed, his ears pricking up. "Did you say 'balloon'?"

"Yes," Piglet said. "But I'm afraid, I'm very sorry, but when I was
running, that is, to bring it, I . . . I . . ."

Piglet's words wound down as he held out what was left of
Eeyore's birthday balloon.

Eeyore took one look and said, "Red. My favorite color. How big
was it?" he couldn't help asking.

"About as big as m-me," Piglet replied.

"My favorite size," Eeyore said wistfully.

Eeyore was sadly eyeing the shredded red balloon when Pooh appeared. "I've brought you a little present, Eeyore," he announced. "It's a useful pot. It's got 'A Very Happy Birthday, with Love from Pooh' written on it. And it's for putting things in."

"Like a balloon?" Eeyore said hopefully.

"Oh, no. Balloons are much too big . . . ," Pooh began, even as Eeyore picked the balloon up with his teeth and dropped it into the very useful pot.

"It *does* fit!" Pooh marveled as Eeyore carefully pulled the balloon out of the pot, then dropped it back in again.

"Eeyore, I'm very glad I thought of giving you a useful pot to put things in," said Pooh.

"And I'm very glad I thought of giving you something to put in a useful pot," said Piglet.

Eeyore didn't say anything. But he looked very, very glad.

It was then that Christopher Robin arrived, along with Owl, Kanga, Roo, Rabbit, and a lovely chocolate birthday cake!

After his friends all sang "Happy Birthday," Eeyore made a wish and blew out the candles. Then Owl clapped his wings and cried, "Bravo! Good show! This reminds me of the party we once gave for my great-uncle Robert. . . ."

Owl had barely begun his story when he was interrupted by a cheerful "Halloo!"

"Oh no! Oh no! Oh no!" cried Rabbit just as Tigger bounced right into him and knocked him to the ground.

"Hello, Tigger," said Roo. "We're having a party."

"A party!" cried Tigger. "Oh boy, oh boy, oh boy. Tiggers love parties." And with no further ado, he bounced over to the table and gobbled up a fistful of cake.

"You've got a lot of nerve showing up here after what you did to Eeyore," Rabbit scolded Tigger. "I think you should leave now."

"Aw, let him stay," cried Roo.

"What do you think, Christopher Robin?" Pooh asked.

"I think," said Christopher Robin, "we all ought to play Pooh Sticks."

And that's exactly what they did.

Eeyore, who had never played the game before, won more times than anybody else. But poor Tigger hadn't won at all.

When it was time for everyone to go home, Tigger threw down his stick and grumbled, "Tiggers don't like Pooh Sticks!" Then, instead of going off in his usual bouncy way, he walked off with his head down and no bounce at all.

"I'd be happy to tell you my secret for winning at Pooh Sticks," Eeyore said, hurrying after Tigger. "It's easy. You just have to let your stick drop in a twitchy sort of way."

"Oh yeah," said Tigger, brightening up immediately. "I forgot to twitch. That was my problem." And then, just because he was feeling so happy, he began bouncing again.

And of course he bounced right into Eeyore.

Meanwhile, Pooh, Piglet, and Christopher Robin lingered on the bridge, quietly watching the peaceful stream.

At last Piglet said, "Tigger's all right, really."

"Of course he is," Christopher Robin agreed.

"Everybody is, really," Pooh mused. "That's what I think." He hesitated a moment, then added, "But I don't suppose I'm right."

"Of course you are," said Christopher Robin, patting Pooh's head. "Silly old bear."